'Alice in Wonderland'

Philosophical Quotes

Lewis Carroll

Selected by Alla Y. Parks

"Begin at the beginning and go on till you come to the end: then stop."

"If everybody minded their own business, the world would go around a great deal faster than it does."

"We're all mad here."

"If you drink much from a bottle marked 'poison' it is certain to disagree with you sooner or later."

"Sometimes I've believed as many as six impossible things before breakfast."

"I don't believe there's an atom of meaning in it."

"Curiouser and curiouser!"

"What is the use of a book, without pictures or conversations?"

"Reeling and Writhing, of course, to begin with, and then the different branches of arithmetic -- Ambition, Distraction, Uglification, and Derision."

"Now, I give you fair warning, either you or your head must be off, and that in about half no time! Take your choice!"

"Sentence first -- verdict afterwards."

"Take care of the sense, and the sounds will take care of themselves."

"Oh my ears and whiskers, how late it's getting!"

"Read the directions and directly you will be directed in the right direction."

"There's a large mustard-mine near here. And the moral of that is -- The more there is of mine, the less there is of yours."

"Well! I've often seen a cat without a grin; but a grin without a cat!"

"Ah! Then yours wasn't a really good school. Now at ours they had at the end of the bill. French, music, and washing -- extra."

"It was much pleasanter at home, when one wasn't always growing larger and smaller, and being ordered about by mice and rabbits."

And she tried to fancy what the flame of a candle is like after the candle is blown out, for she could not remember ever having seen such a thing.

"By-the-bye, what became of the baby?" said the Cat. "I'd nearly forgotten to ask."

"It turned into a pig," Alice quietly said, just as if it had come back in a natural way.

"I thought it would," said the Cat

"Cheshire Puss, would you tell me, please, which way I ought to go from here?"

"That depends a good deal on where you want to get to," said the Cat.

"I don't much care where—"said Alice.

"Then it doesn't matter which way you go," said the Cat.

"--so long as I get somewhere," Alice added as an explanation.

"Oh, you're sure to do that," said the Cat, "if you only walk long enough."

"You've no right to grow here," said the Dormouse.

"Don't talk nonsense," said Alice more boldly: "you know you're growing too."

"Yes, but I grow at a reasonable pace," said the Dormouse: "not in that ridiculous fashion."

"I didn't know that Cheshire cats always grinned; in fact, I didn't know that cats could grin."

"You don't know much," said the Duchess; "and that's a fact."

"No, no! You're a serpent; and there's no use denying it. I suppose you'll be telling me next that you never tasted an egg!"

"Who are you?" said the Caterpillar.

This was not an encouraging opening for a conversation. Alice replied, "I--I hardly know, sir, just at present-- at least I know who I was when I got up this morning, but I think I must have been changed several times since then."

"I wish I hadn't cried so much. I shall be punished for it now, I suppose, by being drowned in my own tears!"

It sounded an excellent plan, no doubt, and very neatly and simply arranged; the only difficulty was, that she had not the smallest idea how to set about it.

"If you're going to turn into a pig, my dear, I'll have nothing more to do with you. Mind now!"

`But I don't want to go among mad people,' Alice remarked.

`Oh, you can't help that,' said the Cat: `we're all mad here. I'm mad. You're mad.'

`How do you know I'm mad?' said Alice.

`You must be,' said the Cat, `or you wouldn't have come here.'

"What a funny watch!" Alice remarked. "It tells the day of the month, and doesn't tell what o'clock it is!"

"Why should it?" muttered the Hatter. "Does your watch tell you what year it is?"

"Of course not," Alice replied very readily: "but that's because it stays the same year for such a long time together."

"Which is just the case with mine," said the Hatter.

"I wish you wouldn't keep appearing and vanishing so suddenly: you make one quite giddy."

"And besides, what would be the use of a procession," thought she, "if people had all to lie down upon their faces, so that they couldn't see it?"

"Have some wine," the March Hare said in an encouraging tone.

Alice looked all-round the table, but there was nothing on it but tea. "I don't see any wine," she remarked.

"There isn't any," said the March Hare.

"Then it wasn't very civil of you to offer it," said Alice angrily.

"It wasn't very civil of you to sit down without being invited," said the March Hare.

"Then you should say what you mean," the March Hare went on.

"I do," Alice hastily replied; "at least--at least I mean what I say--that's the same thing, you know."

"Not the same thing a bit!" said the Hatter. "You might just as well say that "I see what I eat" is the same thing as "I eat what I see"!"

"You might just as well say," added the March Hare, "that "I like what I get" is the same thing as "I get what I like"!"

"You might just as well say," added the Dormouse, who seemed to be talking in his sleep, "that "I breathe when I sleep" is the same thing as "I sleep when I breathe"!"

"What for?" said Alice.

"Did you say "What a pity!"?" the Rabbit asked.

"No, I didn't," said Alice: "I don't think it's at all a pity. I said "What for?"'

"They're dreadfully fond of beheading people here; the great wonder is, that there's any one left alive!"

"It's a friend of mine--a Cheshire Cat," said Alice: "allow me to introduce it."

"I don't like the look of it at all," said the King: "however, it may kiss my hand if it likes."

"A cat may look at a king,"

"Maybe it's always pepper that makes people hot-tempered, and vinegar that makes them sour-- and chamomile that makes them bitter--and--and barley-sugar and such things that make children sweet-tempered.

"I've a right to think," said Alice sharply.

"Just about as much right," said the Duchess, "as pigs have to fly."

"Never imagine yourself not to be otherwise than what it might appear to others that what you were or might have been was not otherwise than what you had been would have appeared to them to be otherwise."

CPSIA information can be obtained at www.ICGtesting.com
Printed in the USA
LVOW10s0033010616

490694LV00031B/833/P